Wilhelm Busch
Max & Moritz
Bilingual Edition
deutsch & english

Max und Moritz

eine

Bubengeschichte

in

sieben Streichen

von

Wilhelm Busch

München,

Verlag von Braun und Schneider.

Titelblatt der Erstauflage von 1865

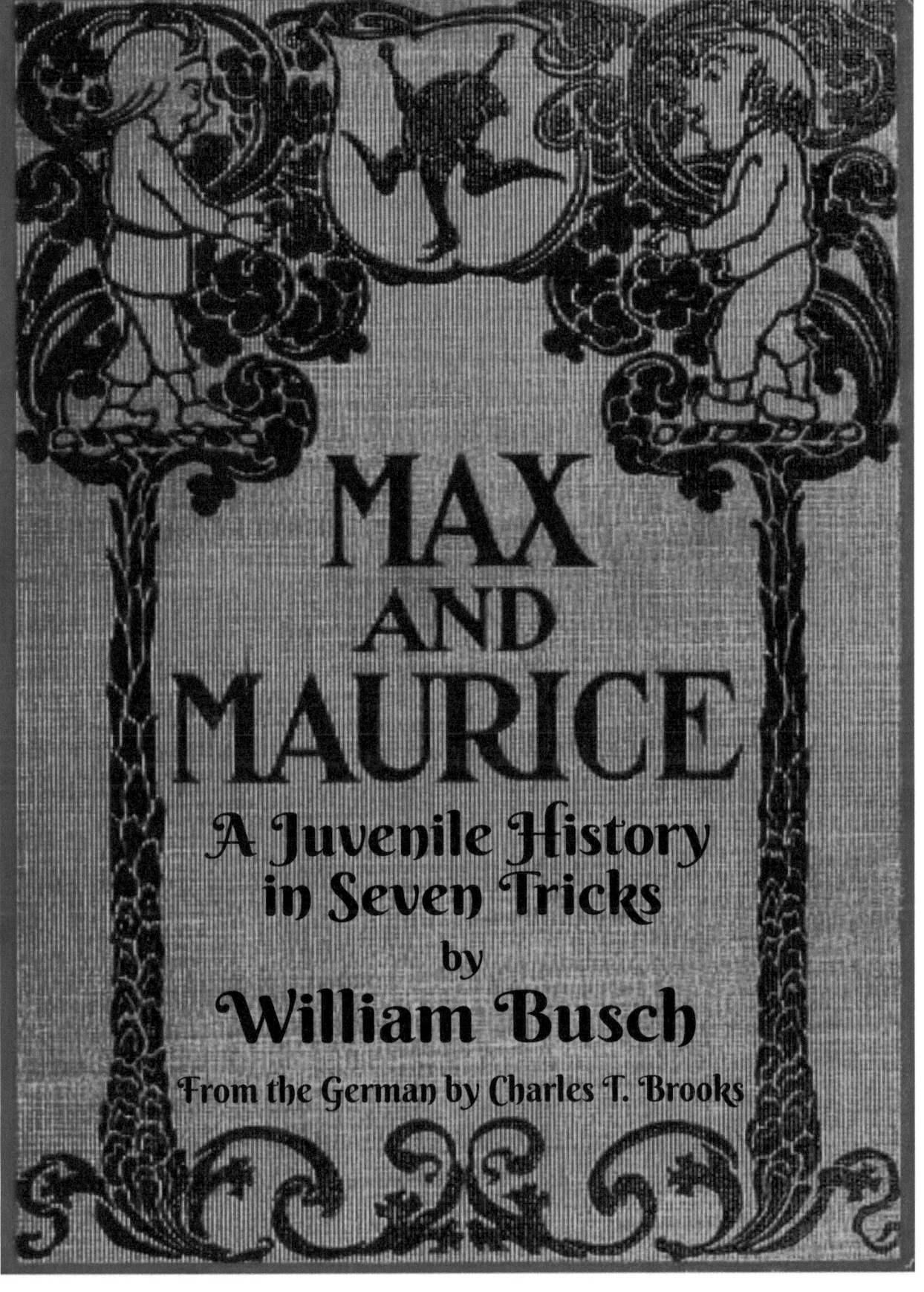

MAX AND MAURICE

A Juvenile History in Seven Tricks

by

William Busch

From the German by Charles T. Brooks

❖

Max & Moritz
deutsch – english
Bilingual Edition

Die Erstauflage von „Max und Moritz" erschien
im Verlag Braun und Schneider, München, 1865.

The English translation by Charles Timothy Brooks was first
published by Braun und Schneider, Munich, in 1871.

Photo Wilhelm Busch 1860: Edgar Hanfstaengl

Übungen zu „Max und Moritz" unter anderem auf:
https://www.grundschulmaterial.de
https://www.lehrer-online.de
https://www.school-scout.de
https://www.lehrerlinks.net
https://www.4teachers.de

Digitale Quelle: Wikisource + Project Gutenberg
http://www.davidgorman.com/maxundmoritz.htm

Satz in Janni-Font: Jan Müller
Druck: Books on Demand GmbH, Norderstedt

Paperback ISBN 978-3-945004-84-5
Paperback full color ISBN 978-3-945004-87-6

❖

Vorwort

Ach, was muss man oft von bösen
Kindern hören oder lesen!
Wie zum Beispiel hier von diesen,
Welche Max und Moritz hießen;

Die, anstatt durch weise Lehren
Sich zum Guten zu bekehren,
Oftmals noch darüber lachten
Und sich heimlich lustig machten. –
Ja, zur Übeltätigkeit,
Ja, dazu ist man bereit! –
Menschen necken, Tiere quälen,
Äpfel, Birnen, Zwetschen stehlen. –
Das ist freilich angenehmer
Und dazu auch viel bequemer,
Als in Kirche oder Schule
Festzusitzen auf dem Stuhle. –
Aber wehe, wehe, wehe!
Wenn ich auf das Ende sehe!! –
Ach, das war ein schlimmes Ding,
Wie es Max und Moritz ging.
Drum ist hier, was sie getrieben,
Abgemalt und aufgeschrieben.

Preface

Ah, how oft we read or hear of
Boys we almost stand in fear of!
For example, take these stories
Of two youths, named Max and Maurice,

Who, instead of early turning
Their young minds to useful learning,
Often leered with horrid features
At their lessons and their teachers.
Look now at the empty head: he
Is for mischief always ready.
Teasing creatures, climbing fences,
Stealing apples, pears, and quinces,
Is, of course, a deal more pleasant,
And far easier for the present,
Than to sit in schools or churches,
Fixed like roosters on their perches.
But O dear, O dear, O deary,
When the end comes sad and dreary!
'Tis a dreadful thing to tell
That on Max and Maurice fell!
All they did this book rehearses,
Both in pictures and in verses.

Erster Streich

Mancher gibt sich viele Müh'
Mit dem lieben Federvieh;
Einesteils der Eier wegen,
Welche diese Vögel legen,
Zweitens: weil man dann und wann
Einen Braten essen kann;
Drittens aber nimmt man auch
Ihre Federn zum Gebrauch
In die Kissen und die Pfühle,
Denn man liegt nicht gerne kühle. –

Trick First

To most people who have leisure
Raising poultry gives great pleasure
First, because the eggs they lay us
For the care we take repay us;
Secondly, that now and then
We can dine on roasted hen;
Thirdly, of the hen's and goose's
Feathers men make various uses.
Some folks like to rest their heads
In the night on feather beds.

Seht, da ist die Witwe Bolte,
Die das auch nicht gerne wollte.

One of these was Widow Tibbets,
Whom the cut you see exhibits.

Ihrer Hühner waren drei
Und ein stolzer Hahn dabei. –

Hens were hers in number three,
And a cock of majesty.

Max und Moritz dachten nun:
Was ist hier jetzt wohl zu tun? –
Ganz geschwinde, eins, zwei, drei,
Schneiden sie sich Brot entzwei,

Max and Maurice took a view;
Fell to thinking what to do.
One, two, three! As soon as said,
They have sliced a loaf of bread,

In vier Teile, jedes Stück
Wie ein kleiner Finger dick.
Diese binden sie an Fäden,
Übers Kreuz, ein Stück an jeden,
Und verlegen sie – genau
In den Hof der guten Frau.

Cut each piece again in four,
Each a finger thick, no more.
These to two cross-threads they tie,
Like a letter X they lie
In the widow's yard, with care
Stretched by those two rascals there.

Kaum hat dies der Hahn gesehen,
Fängt er auch schon an zu krähen:
Kikeriki! Kikikerikih!! –
Tak tak tak! – Da kommen sie.

Scarce the cock had seen the sight,
When he up and crew with might:
Cock-a-doodle-doodle-doo;—
Tack, tack, tack, the trio flew.

Hahn und Hühner schlucken munter
Jedes ein Stück Brot hinunter;

Cock and hens, like fowls unfed,
Gobbled each a piece of bread;

Aber als sie sich besinnen,
Konnte keines recht von hinnen.

But they found, on taking thought,
Each of them was badly caught.

In die Kreuz und in die Quer
Reißen sie sich hin und her,

Every way they pull and twitch,
This strange cat's-cradle to unhitch;

Flattern auf und in die Höh',
Ach herrje, herrjemine!

Up into the air they fly,
Jiminee, O Jimini!

9

Ach, sie bleiben an dem langen
Dürren Ast des Baumes hangen. —
Und ihr Hals wird lang und länger,
Ihr Gesang wird bang und bänger;

On a tree behold them dangling,
In the agony of strangling!
And their necks grow long and longer,
And their groans grow strong and stronger.

Jedes legt noch schnell ein Ei,
Und dann kommt der Tod herbei. —

Each lays quickly one egg more,
Then they cross to th'other shore.

Witwe Bolte, in der Kammer,
Hört im Bette diesen Jammer;

Widow Tibbets in her chamber,
By these death-cries waked from slumber,

Ahnungsvoll tritt sie heraus:
Ach, was war das für ein Graus!

Rushes out with bodeful thought:
Heavens! What sight her vision caught!

„Fließet aus dem Aug', ihr Tränen!
All mein Hoffen, all mein Sehnen,
Meines Lebens schönster Traum
Hängt an diesem Apfelbaum!"

From her eyes the tears are streaming:
»Oh, my cares, my toil, my dreaming!
Ah, life's fairest hope,« says she,
»Hangs upon that apple-tree.«

Tiefbetrübt und sorgenschwer
Kriegt sie jetzt das Messer her;
Nimmt die Toten von den Strängen,
Dass sie so nicht länger hängen,

Heart-sick (you may well suppose),
For the carving-knife she goes;
Cuts the bodies from the bough,
Hanging cold and lifeless now.

Und mit stummem Trauerblick
Kehrt sie in ihr Haus zurück. –

Dieses war der erste Streich,
Doch der zweite folgt sogleich.

And in silence, bathed in tears,
Through her house-door disappears.

This was the bad boys' first trick,
But the second follows quick.

Zweiter Streich

Als die gute Witwe Bolte
Sich von ihrem Schmerz erholte,
Dachte sie so hin und her,
Dass es wohl das Beste wär',
Die Verstorb'nen, die hienieden
Schon so frühe abgeschieden,
Ganz im stillen und in Ehren
Gut gebraten zu verzehren. –
Freilich war die Trauer groß,
Als sie nun so nackt und bloß
Abgerupft am Herde lagen,
Sie, die einst in schönen Tagen
Bald im Hofe, bald im Garten
Lebensfroh im Sande scharrten. ––
Ach, Frau Bolte weint aufs Neu,
Und der Spitz steht auch dabei.

Trick Second

When the worthy Widow Tibbets
(Whom the cut below exhibits)
Had recovered, on the morrow,
From the dreadful shock of sorrow,
She (as soon as grief would let her
Think) began to think 'twere better
Just to take the dead, the dear ones
(Who in life were walking here once),
And in a still noonday hour
Them, well roasted, to devour.
True, it did seem almost wicked,
When they lay so bare and naked,
Picked, and singed before the blaze,—
They that once in happier days,
In the yard or garden ground,
All day long went scratching round.
Ah! Frau Tibbets wept anew,
And poor Spitz was with her, too.

Max und Moritz rochen dieses;
„Schnell aufs Dach gekrochen", hieß es.

Max and Maurice smelt the savor.
»Climb the roof!« cried each young shaver.

Durch den Schornstein mit Vergnügen
Sehen sie die Hühner liegen,
Die schon ohne Kopf und Gurgeln
Lieblich in der Pfanne schmurgeln. –

Through the chimney now, with pleasure,
They behold the tempting treasure,
Headless, in the pan there, lying,
Hissing, browning, steaming, frying.

Eben geht mit einem Teller
Witwe Bolte in den Keller,
Dass sie von dem Sauerkohle
Eine Portion sich hole,
Wofür sie besonders schwärmt,
Wenn er wieder aufgewärmt. –

At that moment down the cellar
(Dreaming not what soon befell her)
Widow Tibbets went for sour
Krout, which she would oft devour
With exceeding great desire
(Warmed a little at the fire).

Unterdessen auf dem Dache
Ist man tätig bei der Sache.
Max hat schon mit Vorbedacht
Eine Angel mitgebracht. –

Up there on the roof, meanwhile,
They are doing things in style.
Max already with forethought
A long fishing-line has brought.

Schnupdiwup! Da wird nach oben
Schon ein Huhn heraufgehoben.
Schnupdiwup! Jetzt Numro zwei;
Schnupdiwup! Jetzt Numro drei;
Und jetzt kommt noch Numro vier:
Schnupdiwup! Dich haben wir! –
Zwar der Spitz sah es genau,
Und er bellt: Rawau! Rawau!

Schnupdiwup! There goes, O Jeminy!
One hen dangling up the chimney.
Schnupdiwup! A second bird!
Schnupdiwup! Up comes the third!
Presto! Number four they haul!
Schnupdiwup! We have them all!—
Spitz looks on, we must allow,
But he barks: Row-wow! Row-wow!

Aber schon sind sie ganz munter
Fort und von dem Dach herunter. —

But the rogues are down instanter
From the roof, and off they canter.—

Na! Das wird Spektakel geben,
Denn Frau Bolte kommt soeben;
Angewurzelt stand sie da,
Als sie nach der Pfanne sah.

Ha! I guess there'l be a humming;
Here's the Widow Tibbets coming!
Rooted stood she to the spot,
When the pan her vision caught.

Alle Hühner waren fort. –
„Spitz!" – Das war ihr erstes Wort. –

Gone was every blessed bird!
»Horrid Spitz!« was her first word.

„Oh, du Spitz, du Ungetüm! –
Aber wart! Ich komme ihm!!"

»O you Spitz, you monster, you!
Let me beat him black and blue!«

Mit dem Löffel groß und schwer,
Geht es über Spitzen her;
Laut ertönt sein Wehgeschrei,
Denn er fühlt sich schuldenfrei. —

And the heavy ladle, thwack!
Comes down on poor Spitz's back!
Loud he yells with agony,
For he feels his conscience free.

Max und Moritz, im Verstecke,
Schnarchen aber an der Hecke,
Und vom ganzen Hühnerschmaus
Guckt nur noch ein Bein heraus. —

Dieses war der zweite Streich,
Doch der dritte folgt sogleich.

Max and Maurice, dinner over,
In a hedge, snored under cover;
And of that great hen-feast now
Each has but a leg to show

This was now the second trick,
But the third will follow quick.

Dritter Streich

Jedermann im Dorfe kannte
Einen, der sich Böck benannte. –

Alltagsröcke, Sonntagsröcke,
Lange Hosen, spitze Fräcke,
Westen mit bequemen Taschen,
Warme Mäntel und Gamaschen –
Alle diese Kleidungssachen
Wusste Schneider Böck zu machen. –
Oder wäre was zu flicken,
Abzuschneiden, anzustücken,
Oder gar ein Knopf der Hose
Abgerissen oder lose –
Wie und wo und was es sei,
Hinten, vorne, einerlei –
Alles macht der Meister Böck,
Denn das ist sein Lebenszweck. –
Drum so hat in der Gemeinde
Jedermann ihn gern zum Freunde. –
Aber Max und Moritz dachten,
Wie sie ihn verdrießlich machten. –

Trick Third

Through the town and country round
Was one Mr. Buck renowned.

Sunday coats, and week-day sack-coats,
Bob-tails, swallow-tails, and frock coats,
Gaiters, breeches, hunting-jackets;
Waistcoats, with commodious pockets,—
And other things, too long to mention,
Claimed Mr. Tailor Buck's attention.
Or, if any thing wanted doing
In the way of darning, sewing,
Piecing, patching,—if a button
Needed to be fixed or put on,—
Any thing of any kind,
Anywhere, before, behind,—
Master Buck could do the same,
For it was his life's great aim.
Therefore all the population
Held him high in estimation.
Max and Maurice tried to invent
Ways to plague this worthy gent.

Námlich vor des Meisters Hause
Floss ein Wasser mit Gebrause.

Right before the Sartor's dwelling
Ran a swift stream, roaring, swelling.

Übers Wasser führt ein Steg
Und darüber geht der Weg. —

This swift stream a bridge did span,
And the road across it ran.

Max und Moritz, gar nicht träge,
Sägen heimlich mit der Säge —
Ritzeratze! – voller Tücke
In die Brücke eine Lücke. —

Max and Maurice (naught could awe them!)
Took a saw, when no one saw them:
Ritze-ratze! riddle-diddle!
Sawed a gap across the middle.

Als nun diese Tat vorbei,
Hört man plötzlich ein Geschrei:

When this feat was finished well,
Suddenly was heard a yell:

„He, heraus! Du Ziegen-Böck!
Schneider, Schneider, meck, meck, meck!!"
Alles konnte Böck ertragen,
Ohne nur ein Wort zu sagen;
Aber wenn er dies erfuhr,
Ging's ihm wider die Natur. —

»Hallo, there! Come out, you buck!
Tailor, Tailor, muck! muck! muck!«
Buck could bear all sorts of jeering,
Jibes and jokes in silence hearing;
But this insult roused such anger,
Nature couldn't stand it longer.

Schnelle springt er mit der Elle
Über seines Hauses Schwelle,
Denn schon wieder ihm zum Schreck
Tönt ein lautes: „Meck, meck, meck!!"

Wild with fury, up he started,
With his yard-stick out he darted;
For once more that frightful jeer,
»Muck! muck! muck!« rang loud and clear.

Und schon ist er auf der Brücke,
Kracks! Die Brücke bricht in Stücke;

On the bridge one leap he makes;
Crash! Beneath his weight it breaks.

Wieder tónt es: „Meck, meck, meck!"
Plumps! Da ist der Schneider weg!

Once more rings the cry, »Muck! muck!«
In, headforemost, plumps poor Buck!

Grad als dieses vorgekommen,
Kommt ein Gänsepaar geschwommen,
Welches Böck in Todeshast
Krampfhaft bei den Beinen faßt.

While the scared boys were skedaddling,
Down the brook two geese came paddling.
On the legs of these two geese,
With a death-clutch, Buck did seize;

Beide Gänse in der Hand,
Flattert er auf trocknes Land. —

And, with both geese well in hand,
Flutters out upon dry land.

Übrigens bei alledem
Ist so etwas nicht bequem;

For the rest he did not find
Things exactly to his mind.

Wie denn Böck von der Geschichte
Auch das Magendrücken kriegte.

Soon it proved poor Buck had brought a
Dreadful belly-ache from the water.

Hoch ist hier Frau Böck zu preisen!
Denn ein heißes Bügeleisen,
Auf den kalten Leib gebracht,
Hat es wieder gut gemacht. –

Noble Mrs. Buck! She rises
Fully equal to the crisis;
With a hot flat-iron, she
Draws the cold out famously.

Bald im Dorf hinauf, hinunter,
Hieß es: Böck ist wieder munter! –
Dieses war der dritte Streich,
Doch der vierte folgt sogleich.

Soon ›twas in the mouths of men,
All through town: »Buck's up again!«
This was the bad boys' third trick,
But the fourth will follow quick.

Vierter Streich

Also lautet ein Beschluss:
Dass der Mensch was lernen muss. –
Nicht allein das A-B-C
Bringt den Menschen in die Höh';
Nicht allein im Schreiben, Lesen
Übt sich ein vernünftig Wesen;
Nicht allein in Rechnungssachen
Soll der Mensch sich Mühe machen;
Sondern auch der Weisheit Lehren
Muss man mit Vergnügen hören. –

Trick Fourth

An old saw runs somewhat so:
Man must learn while here below.—
Not alone the A, B, C,
Raises man in dignity;
Not alone in reading, writing,
Reason finds a work inviting;
Not alone to solve the double
Rule of Three shall man take trouble:
But must hear with pleasure Sages
Teach the wisdom of the ages.

Dass dies mit Verstand geschah,
War Herr Lehrer Lämpel da. –

Max und Moritz, diese beiden,
Mochten ihn darum nicht leiden;
Denn wer böse Streiche macht,
Gibt nicht auf den Lehrer acht. –

Of this wisdom an example
To the world was Master Lämpel.

For this cause, to Max and Maurice
This man was the chief of horrors;
For a boy who loves bad tricks
Wisdom's friendship never seeks.

Nun war dieser brave Lehrer
Von dem Tobak ein Verehrer,
Was man ohne alle Frage
Nach des Tages Müh und Plage
Einem guten, alten Mann
Auch von Herzen gönnen kann. –

Max und Moritz, unverdrossen,
Sinnen aber schon auf Possen,
Ob vermittelst seiner Pfeifen
Dieser Mann nicht anzugreifen.

With the clerical profession
Smoking always was a passion;
And this habit without question,
While it helps promote digestion,
Is a comfort no one can
Well begrudge a good old man,
When the day's vexations close,
And he sits to seek repose.—
Max and Maurice, flinty-hearted,
On another trick have started;
Thinking how they may attack a
Poor old man through his tobacco.

Einstens, als es Sonntag wieder
Und Herr Lämpel brav und bieder
In der Kirche mit Gefühle
Saß vor seinem Orgelspiele,

Once, when Sunday morning breaking,
Pious hearts to gladness waking,
Poured its light where, in the temple
At his organ sat Herr Lämpel,

Schlichen sich die bösen Buben
In sein Haus und seine Stuben,
Wo die Meerschaumpfeife stand;
Max hält sie in seiner Hand;

These bad boys, for mischief ready,
Stole into the good man's study,
Where his darling meerschaum stands.
This, Max holds in both his hands;

Aber Moritz aus der Tasche
Zieht die Flintenpulverflasche,
Und geschwinde, stopf, stopf, stopf!
Pulver in den Pfeifenkopf. -
Jetzt nur still und schnell nach Haus,
Denn schon ist die Kirche aus. -

While young Maurice (scapegrace born!)
Climbs, and gets the powderhorn,
And with speed the wicked soul
Pours the powder in the bowl.
Hush, and quick! Now, right about!
For already church is out.

Eben schließt in sanfter Ruh'
Lämpel seine Kirche zu;

Lämpel closes the church-door,
Glad to seek his home once more;

Und mit Buch und Notenheften,
Nach besorgten Amtsgeschäften,

All his service well got through,
Takes his keys, and music too,

Lenkt er freudig seine Schritte
Zu der heimatlichen Hütte,

And his way, delighted, wends
Homeward to his silent friends.

Und voll Dankbarkeit sodann,
Zündet er sein Pfeifchen an.

Full of gratitude he there
Lights his pipe, and takes his chair.

„Ach!" - spricht er - „die größte Freud'
Ist doch die Zufriedenheit!!"

»Ah!« he says, »no joy is found
Like contentment on earth's round!«

Rums! - Da geht die Pfeife los
Mit Getöse, schrecklich groß.
Kaffeetopf und Wasserglas,
Tobaksdose, Tintenfass,
Ofen, Tisch und Sorgensitz,
Alles fliegt im Pulverblitz.

Fizz! whizz! bum! The pipe is burst,
Almost shattered into dust.
Coffee-pot and water-jug,
Snuff-box, ink-stand, tumbler, mug,
Table, stove, and easy-chair,
All are flying through the air
In a lightning-powder-flash,
With a most tremendous crash.

Als der Dampf sich nun erhob,
Sieht man Lämpel, der – gottlob! –
Lebend auf dem Rücken liegt;
Doch er hat was abgekriegt.

When the smoke-cloud lifts and clears,
Lämpel on his back appears;
God be praised! – still breathing there,
Only somewhat worse for wear.

Nase, Hand, Gesicht und Ohren
Sind so schwarz als wie die Mohren,
Und des Haares letzter Schopf
Ist verbrannt bis auf den Kopf. –

Nose, hands, eyebrows (once like yours),
Now are black as any Moor's;
Burned the last thin spear of hair,
And his pate is wholly bare.

Wer soll nun die Kinder lehren
Und die Wissenschaft vermehren?
Wer soll nun für Lämpel leiten
Seine Amtestätigkeiten?
Woraus soll der Lehrer rauchen,
Wenn die Pfeife nicht zu brauchen??

Who shall now the children guide,
Lead their steps to wisdom's side?
Who shall now for Master Lämpel
Lead the service in the temple?
Now that his old pipe is out,
Shattered, smashed, gone up the spout?

Mit der Zeit wird alles heil,
Nur die Pfeife hat ihr Teil. —

Time will heal the rest once more,
But the pipe's best days are o'er.

Dieses war der vierte Streich,
Doch der fünfte folgt sogleich.

This was the bad boys' fourth trick,
But the fifth will follow quick.

Fünfter Streich

Wer in Dorfe oder Stadt
Einen Onkel wohnen hat,
Der sei höflich und bescheiden,
Denn das mag der Onkel leiden.

Morgens sagt man: „Guten Morgen!
Haben Sie was zu besorgen?"
Bringt ihm, was er haben muss:
Zeitung, Pfeife, Fidibus.

Oder sollt' es wo im Rücken
Drücken, beißen oder zwicken,
Gleich ist man mit Freudigkeit
Dienstbeflissen und bereit.

Oder sei's nach einer Prise,
Dass der Onkel heftig niese,
Ruft man „Prosit!" alsogleich,
„Danke! Wohl bekomm' es Euch!"

Oder kommt er spät nach Haus,
Zieht man ihm die Stiefel aus,
Holt Pantoffel, Schlafrock, Mütze,
Dass er nicht im Kalten sitze.

Kurz, man ist darauf bedacht,
Was dem Onkel Freude macht.

Max und Moritz ihrerseits
Fanden darin keinen Reiz.
Denkt euch nur, welch schlechten Witz
Machten sie mit Onkel Fritz!

Trick Fifth

If, in village or in town,
You've an uncle settled down,
Always treat him courteously;
Uncle will be pleased thereby.

In the morning: »Morning to you!
Any errand I can do you?«
Fetch whatever he may need,
Pipe to smoke, and news to read;

Or should some confounded thing
Prick his back, or bite, or sting,
Nephew then will be near by,
Ready to his help to fly;

Or a pinch of snuff, maybe,
Sets him sneezing violently:
»Prosit! Uncle! Good health to you!
God be praised! Much good may't do you!«

Or he comes home late, perchance:
Pull his boots off then at once,
Fetch his slippers and his cap,
And warm gown his limbs to wrap.

Be your constant care, good boy,
What shall give your uncle joy.

Max and Maurice (need I mention?)
Had not any such intention.
See now how they tried their wits—
These bad boys—on Uncle Fritz.

Jeder weiß, was so ein Mai-
Käfer für ein Vogel sei.

What kind of a bird a May-
Bug was, they knew, I dare say;

In den Bäumen hin und her
Fliegt und kriecht und krabbelt er.

In the trees they may be found,
Flying, crawling, wriggling round.

Max und Moritz, immer munter,
Schütteln sie vom Baum herunter.

Max and Maurice, great pains taking,
From a tree these bugs are shaking.

In die Tüte von Papiere
Sperren sie die Krabbeltiere. —

In their cornucopiæ papers,
They collect these pinching creepers.

Fort damit, und in die Ecke
Unter Onkel Fritzens Decke!

Soon they are deposited
In the foot of uncle's bed!

Bald zu Bett geht Onkel Fritze
In der spitzen Zippelmütze;

With his peaked nightcap on,
Uncle Fritz to bed has gone;

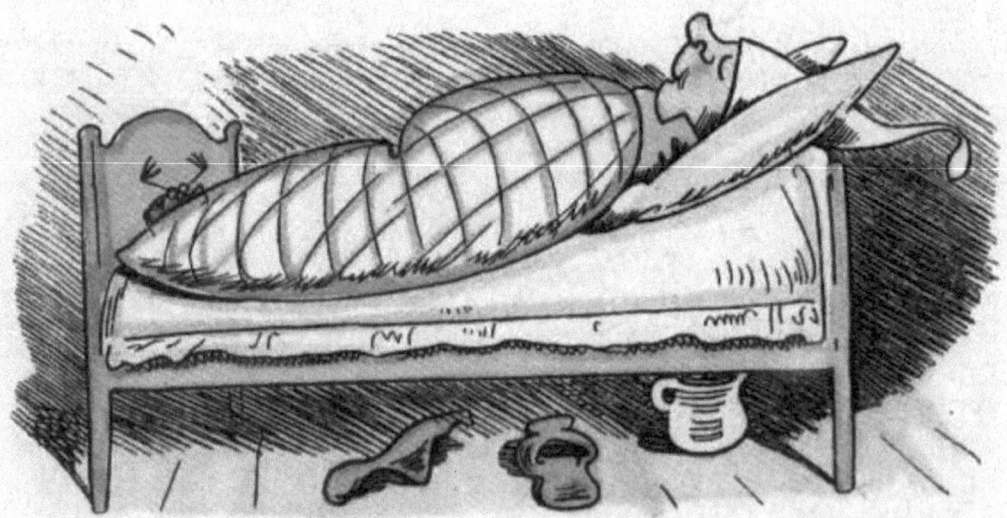

Seine Augen macht er zu,
Hüllt sich ein und schläft in Ruh.

Tucks the clothes in, shuts his eyes,
And in sweetest slumber lies.

Doch die Käfer, kritze kratze!
Kommen schnell aus der Matratze.

Kritze! Kratze! Come the Tartars
Single file from their night quarters.

Schon fasst einer, der voran,
Onkel Fritzens Nase an.

And the captain boldly goes
Straight at Uncle Fritzy's nose.

„Bau!" - schreit er - „Was ist das hier?"
Und erfasst das Ungetier.

»Baugh!« he cries: »What have we here?«
Seizing that grim grenadier.

Und den Onkel, voller Grausen,
Sieht man aus dem Bette sausen.

Uncle, wild with fright, upspringeth,
And the bedclothes from him flingeth.

„Autsch!" - Schon wieder hat er einen
Im Genicke, an den Beinen;

»Awtsch!« he seizes two more scape-
Graces from his shin and nape.

Hin und her und rund herum
Kriecht es, fliegt es mit Gebrumm.

Crawling, flying, to and fro,
Round the buzzing rascals go.

Onkel Fritz, in dieser Not,
Haut und trampelt alles tot

Wild with fury, Uncle Fritz
Stamps and slashes them to bits.

Guckste wohl! Jetzt ist's vorbei
Mit der Käferkrabbelei!

O be joyful! All gone by
Is the May bug's deviltry.

Onkel Fritz hat wieder Ruh'
Und macht seine Augen zu. –

Dieses war der fünfte Streich,
Doch der sechste folgt sogleich.

Uncle Fritz his eyes can close
Once again in sweet repose.

This was the bad boys' fifth trick,
But the sixth will follow quick.

Sechster Streich

In der schönen Osterzeit,
Wenn die frommen Bäckersleut',
Viele süße Zuckersachen
Backen und zurechtemachen,
Wünschten Max und Moritz auch
Sich so etwas zum Gebrauch. –

Trick Sixth

Easter days have come again,
When the pious baker men
Bake all sorts of sugar things,
Plum-cakes, ginger-cakes, and rings.
Max and Maurice feel an ache
In their sweet-tooth for some cake.

Doch der Bäcker, mit Bedacht,
Hat das Backhaus zugemacht.

But the Baker thoughtfully
Locks his shop, and takes the key.

Also, will hier einer stehlen,
Muss er durch den Schlot sich quälen. –

Who would steal, then, this must do:
Wriggle down the chimney-flue.

Ratsch! – Da kommen die zwei Knaben   Ratsch! There come the boys, my Jiminy!
Durch den Schornstein, schwarz wie Raben.   Black as ravens, down the chimney.

Puff! – Sie fallen in die Kist',   Puff! into a chest they drop,
Wo das Mehl darinnen ist.   Full of flour up to the top.

Da! Nun sind sie alle beide
Rund herum so weiß wie Kreide.

Out they crawl from under cover
Just as white as chalk all over.

Aber schon mit viel Vergnügen
Sehen sie die Brezeln liegen.

But the cracknels, precious treasure,
On a shelf they spy with pleasure.

Knacks!! - Da bricht der Stuhl entzwei;   Knacks! The chair breaks! Down they go—

Schwapp!! - Da liegen sie im Brei.   Schwapp!—into a trough of dough!

| Ganz von Kuchenteig umhüllt | All enveloped now in dough, |
| Stehn sie da als Jammerbild. – | See them, monuments of woe. |

| Gleich erscheint der Meister Bäcker | In the Baker comes, and snickers |
| Und bemerkt die Zuckerlecker. | When he sees the sugar-lickers. |

Eins, zwei, drei! - Eh' man's gedacht,
Sind zwei Brote draus gemacht.

One, two, three! The brats, behold!
Into two good brots are rolled.

In dem Ofen glüht es noch -
Ruff! - Damit ins Ofenloch!

There's the oven, all red-hot,—
Shove ›em in as quick as thought.

Ruff! - Man zieht sie aus der Glut, –
Denn nun sind sie braun und gut. –

Ruff! Out with ›em from the heat,
They are brown and good to eat.

Jeder denkt: „Die sind perdú!"
Aber nein! – Noch leben sie! –

Now you think they've paid the debt!
No, my friend, they're living yet.

Knusper, knasper! - Wie zwei Mäuse
Fressen sie durch das Gehäuse;

Knusper! Knasper! Like two mice
Through their roofs they gnaw in a trice;

Und der Meister Bäcker schrie:
»Ach, herrjeh! Da laufen sie!«
Dieses war der sechste Streich,
Doch der letzte folgt sogleich.

And the Baker cries, »You bet!
There's the rascals living yet!«
This was the bad boys' sixth trick,
But the last will follow quick.

Letzter Streich

Last Trick

Max und Moritz, wehe euch!
Jetzt kommt euer letzter Streich!

Max and Maurice! I grow sick,
When I think on your last trick.

Wozu müssen auch die beiden
Löcher in die Säcke schneiden?? –

Why must these two scalawags
Cut those gashes in the bags?

Seht, da trägt der Bauer Mecke
Einen seiner Maltersäcke. —

See! The farmer on his back
Carries corn off in a sack.

Aber kaum dass er von hinnen,
Fängt das Korn schon an zu rinnen.

Scarce has he begun to travel,
When the corn runs out like gravel.

Und verwundert steht und spricht er:
„Zapperment! Dat Ding werd lichter!"

All at once he stops and cries:
»Darn it! I see where it lies!«

Hei! Da sieht er voller Freude
Max und Moritz im Getreide.

Ha! With what delighted eyes
Max and Maurice he espies.

Rabs! - In seinen großen Sack
Schaufelt er das Lumpenpack.

Rabs! He opens wide his sack,
Shoves the rogues in—Hukepack!

Max und Moritz wird es schwűle,
Denn nun geht es nach der Műhle. —

It grows warm with Max and Maurice,
For to mill the farmer hurries.

„Meister Műller, he, heran!
Mahl' er das, so schnell er kann!"

»Master Miller! Hallo, man!
Grind me that as quick as you can!«

„Her damit!" – Und in den Trichter
Schüttelt er die Bösewichter. –

»In with 'em!« Each wretched flopper
Headlong goes into the hopper.

Rickeracke! Rickeracke!
Geht die Mühle mit Geknacke.

As the farmer turns his back, he
Hears the mill go »creaky! cracky!«

Hier kann man sie noch erblicken
Fein geschroten und in Stücken.

Here you see the bits post mortem,
Just as Fate was pleased to sort 'em.

Doch sogleich verzehret sie
Meister Müllers Federvieh. –

Master Miller's ducks with speed
Gobbled up the coarse-grained feed.

Schluss

Als man dies im Dorf erfuhr,
War von Trauer keine Spur. –
Witwe Bolte, mild und weich,
Sprach: „Sieh da, ich dacht es gleich!" –
„Ja ja ja!" rief Meister Böck,
„Bosheit ist kein Lebenszweck!" –
Drauf so sprach Herr Lehrer Lämpel:
„Dies ist wieder ein Exempel!" –
„Freilich!" meint der Zuckerbäcker,
„Warum ist der Mensch so lecker?!" –
Selbst der gute Onkel Fritze
Sprach: „Das kommt von dumme Witze!" –
Doch der brave Bauersmann
Dachte: „Wat geiht meck dat an?!" –
Kurz, im ganzen Ort herum
Ging ein freudiges Gebrumm:
„Gott sei Dank! Nun ist's vorbei
Mit der Übeltäterei!!"

Conclusion

In the village not a word,
Not a sign, of grief, was heard.
Widow Tibbets, speaking low,
Said, »I thought it would be so!«
»None but self,« cried Buck, »to blame!
Mischief is not life's true aim!«
Then said gravely Teacher Lämpel,
»There again is an example!«
»To be sure! bad thing for youth,«
Said the Baker, »a sweet tooth!«
Even Uncle says, »Good folks!
See what comes of stupid jokes!«
But the honest farmer: »Guy!
What concern is that to I?«
Through the place in short there went
One wide murmur of content:
»God be praised! The town is free
From this great rascality!«

Nachwort

Ja, mit der Übeltäterei ist's nun vorbei, aber noch lange nicht mit Max und Moritz. Wir haben ja schon beim Bäcker gesehen, dass selbst die Backofenhitze den beiden nichts anhaben kann:

Jeder denkt, sie sind perdü, aber nein, noch leben sie!

Spätestens da wurde uns klar, dass Max und Moritz keine normalen Sterblichen sind, sondern Geschöpfe des Geistes, deren Name und Form in der Erinnerung weiterleben – bis auf den heutigen Tag. Betrachten wir einmal, wann und wie sie im Kopf ihres Schöpfers entstanden, wie sie das Licht der Welt erblickten, die Kinderherzen auf der ganzen Welt eroberten und es schließlich bis zu Film-, Ballett- und Bühnenstars brachten.

In seinen ersten Lebensjahren bei seinen Eltern in Wiedensahl war Wilhelm Busch nach eigenen Aussagen keineswegs ein Lausbub, sondern eher ein empfindsames, ängstliches Kind. Die Geschichte von Max und Moritz beginnt erst im Herbst 1841, als er mit neun Jahren zu seinem Onkel Georg Kleine kam, dem Pfarrer von Ebergötzen. Von ihm bekam er Privatunterricht, an dem auch sein neuer Freund Erich Bachmann teilnahm, der Sohn des Müllers.

Schon im Kindesalter hatte Wilhelm Busch großes Zeichentalent bewiesen. Mit 14 Jahren zeichnete er seinen Freund Erich als pausbäckigen, selbstbewussten Jungen von kräftiger Struktur wie Max und sich selbst mit einer Frisur, die erste Ähnlichkeit mit Moritz zeigt. Eine spätere Karikatur von sich macht aus seinem Haarwirbel bereits die kesse Tolle, die später zum Markenzeichen von Moritz werden sollte.

Epilogue

Yes, from rascality the town is free, but not at all from Max and Maurice. We've already seen at the bakery that even the heat of the oven couldn't harm them:

Now you think they've paid the debt! No, my friend, they're living yet.

At the latest then it became clear to us that Max and Maurice are no normal mortals, but creatures of the mind, whose name and form survive in our memory – up to the present day.

Let's take a look at when and how they came into being in the mind of their creator, how they saw the light of day, conquered the hearts of children all over the world and finally made it to film, ballet and stage stars.

In the first years of his life with his parents in Wiedensahl, William Busch was, according to his own statements, by no means a rascal, but rather a sensitive, anxious child.

The story of Max and Maurice does not begin until the fall of 1841, when at the age of nine he came to live with his uncle Georg Kleine, the pastor of Ebergötzen. From him he received private lessons, which were also attended by his new friend Erich Bachmann, the son of the miller.

William Busch had already shown great talent for drawing in his childhood.

At the age of 14 he drew his friend Erich as a chubby, self-confident boy of strong structure like Max and himself with a hairstyle that shows the first resemblance to Maurice.

A later caricature of himself already turns his twirl of hair into the perky quiff that would later become Maurice's trademark.

Auf die Frage nach dem Wahrheitsgehalt der Streiche antwortete er später: »Du fragst, ob Max und Moritz eine wahre Geschichte sei. Nun, so ganz wohl nicht. Das meiste ist bloß so ausgedacht, aber einiges ist wirklich passiert. Und dass böse Streiche kein gutes Ende nehmen, da wird sicher was Wahres dran sein.«

Die beiden Freunde liefen zum Beispiel weiß bemehlt in der Bachmannschen Mühle umher oder zogen sich bei schönem Wetter am Ufer der Aue aus und überkleisterten sich mit Schlamm, um sich anschließend in der Sonne trocknen zu lassen.

When asked later about the truth of the pranks, he replied: »You ask whether Max and Maurice is a true story. Well, not quite. Most of it is just made up, but some of it really happened. And that evil pranks don't have good endings, there's bound to be some truth to that.«

The two friends, for example, walked around the Bachmann mill covered in white flour or, in fine weather, undressed on the banks of the river Aue and covered themselves with mud, then let themselves dry in the sun.

Das Haus der Witwe Bolte und der Steg, über den Schneider Böck ging, waren in unmittelbarer Nachbarschaft der Mühle. Schneider waren beliebte Ziele für Karikatur und Spott. Sie galten als unmännlich und unrein. Auch einen Lehrer Lämpel hatte Ebergötzen zu bieten.

The house of Widow Tibbets and the footbridge over which Tailor Buck walked were in the immediate vicinity of the mill. Tailors were popular figures in caricatures and mockery. They were considered unmanly, dishonest and impure. Ebergötzen also had a Master Lämpel.

Dorflehrer wurden miserabel bezahlt und hatten Zusatzpflichten wie Kantor- und Küsterdienste wahrzunehmen.

Village teachers were miserably paid and had to perform additional duties such as cantor and sexton services.

In der Mühle, in der Max und Moritz zermahlen werden, »... die mich seit Kinderzeiten immer freundlich aufgenommen hat ...«, haben Erich und Wilhelm ihre lebenslange Freundschaft immer wieder erneuert.

Noch heute wird dort wie in alter Zeit Korn geschrotet und zu Mehl gemahlen. Das schwere Mühlrad treibt wie seit Jahrhunderten das Zahnradgetriebe an.

»Das Bett wackelte beim Getriebe der Räder, und das herabstürzende Wasser rauschte durch meine Träume«, so beschrieb Wilhelm Busch seine Nächte in der Mühle.

Heute beherbergt die Wilhelm-Busch-Mühle in Ebergötzen eine Ausstellung mit Max-und-Moritz-Übersetzungen aus fast allen Winkeln der Welt.

In the mill where Max and Maurice are ground, »... which has always received me kindly since childhood ...«, Erich and William have renewed their lifelong friendship again and again.

Even today, as in ancient times, grain is ground there and milled into flour. The heavy mill wheel drives the gear train, as it has for centuries.

»The bed shook at the gearing of the wheels, and the falling water rushed through my dreams«, is how William Busch described his nights in the mill.

Today, the Wilhelm-Busch-Mill in Ebergötzen houses an exhibition of Max and Maurice translations from almost every corner of the world.

Das sind die Anregungen aus dem wirklichen Leben. Die Idee für den ersten und dritten Streich fand Wilhelm Busch in dem 1515 anonym erschienenen Volksbuch »Ein kurzweilig Lesen von Till Eulenspiegel aus dem Lande zu Braunschweig«, wo es heißt:

Die achte Historie sagt, wie Eulenspiegel die Hühner des geizigen Bauern dazu brachte, sich um die Köder zu reißen.

Eulenspiegel ... knüpfte zwanzig Fäden oder mehr je zwei und zwei in der Mitte zu einem Fadenkreuz zusammen und band an jedes Fadenende einen Bissen Brot und legte die Fäden verdeckt hin, nur die Brotstücke waren zu sehen. Die Hühner pickten nun hier und dort die Brotbissen an den Fäden und schluckten sie in ihre Hälse, aber sie konnten sie nicht herunterschlucken ...

These are the inspirations from real life. William Busch found the idea for the first and third prank in the folk book »A diverting read of Dyl Ulenspiegel, born in the land of Brunswick, how he spent his life" published in 1515, where it says:

The eighth history tells how Ulenspiegel made the miserly farmer's chickens scramble for bait.

Ulenspiegel ... tied twenty threads or more, two at a time and two in the middle to form a cross and tied a morsel of bread to each end of the thread and placed the threads under cover so that only the pieces of bread were visible. The chickens now pecked here and there the bread bites at the threads and swallowed them into their necks, but they could not swallow them ...

Die zweiunddreißigste Historie sagt, wie Eulenspiegel die Stadtwachen in Nürnberg dazu brachte, ihm über einen Steg zu folgen, sodass sie ins Wasser fielen. Eulenspiegel ... brach aus dem Steg drei Bohlen und warf sie ins Wasser. Und er ging vor das Rathaus und begann zu fluchen ... Als die Wächter das hörten, waren sie schnell auf den Beinen und liefen ihm nach ...

The thirty-second history tells how Ulenspiegel made the city guards in Nuremberg follow him over a footbridge so that they fell into the water.

Ulenspiegel broke three planks from the footbridge and threw them into the water. And he went in front of the town hall and began to curse ... When the guards heard this, they were quickly on their feet and ran after him ...

Aus diesen Eulenspiegelstreichen entstanden die ersten drei Max-und-Moritz-Streiche, da Wilhelm Busch inzwischen gewohnt war, als Brotberuf satirische Karikaturen und Bildergeschichten herzustellen.

Nach einem abgebrochenen Kunststudium in Düsseldorf und Antwerpen war er nach München gezogen, hatte im Künstlerverein Jung München die dortige Kunstszene kennengelernt und für die Vereinszeitung Karikaturen und Gebrauchstexte beigetragen.

Dadurch war Kaspar Braun, der Verleger der satirischen Zeitungen Münchener Bilderbogen und Fliegende Blätter, auf ihn aufmerksam geworden und hatte ihm eine freie Mitarbeit angeboten. Zwischen 1859 und 1863 verfasste Wilhelm Busch über hundert Beiträge für den Münchener Bilderbogen und die Fliegenden Blätter.

These Ulenspiegel pranks gave rise to the first three Max and Maurice tricks, after William Busch had by then become accustomed to producing satirical caricatures and picture stories as his bread and butter.

After abandoning his art studies in Düsseldorf and Antwerp, he had moved to Munich, got to know the local art scene in the artists' association Jung München and contributed caricatures and commercial texts to the association's newspaper.

This brought him to the attention of Kaspar Braun, the publisher of the satirical newspapers Münchener Bilderbogen and Fliegende Blätter, who offered him a freelance position.

Between 1859 and 1863, William Busch wrote over a hundred articles for the Münchener Bilderbogen and the Fliegende Blätter.

Die Abhängigkeit von seinem Verleger Kaspar Braun fand Busch jedoch beengend, sodass er sich in Heinrich Richter einen neuen Verleger suchte. Da bei Richter Kinderbücher und religiöse Erbauungsliteratur erschienen, vereinbarte er mit ihm die Publikation eines Bilderbuchs. Seine vier vorgeschlagenen »Bilderpossen« stießen jedoch bei Richter auf Vorbehalte. Noch

However, Busch found the dependence on his publisher Kaspar Braun restrictive, so he looked for a new publisher in Heinrich Richter. Since Richter published children's books and religious edification literature, he agreed with him to publish a picture book. His four proposed »Bilderpossen« met with Richter's reservations, however.

während die Bilderpossen für den Druck vorbereitet wurden, begann Wilhelm Busch im November 1863 an Max und Moritz zu arbeiten.

Am 12. Dezember hatte er rund hundert Zeichnungen fertig, damals noch ohne Verse, die er immer erst nach den Zeichnungen schrieb. Als sich die Bilderpossen als Misserfolg herausstellten, bot er Heinrich Richter im Oktober 1864, wahrscheinlich als Wiedergutmachung für den erlittenen finanziellen Verlust, das Manuskript von Max und Moritz zur Veröffentlichung an und verzichtete dabei auf jegliche Honorarforderung.

Heinrich Richter lehnte das Manuskript jedoch ab, nachdem auch sein Vater Ludwig Richter zu dem Urteil gekommen war, dass Leute, die an so etwas Vergnügen hätten, keine Bücher kaufen würden. Also wandte sich Wilhelm Busch am 5. Februar 1865 wieder an seinen alten Verleger Kaspar Braun:

While the Bilderpossen were still being prepared for printing, William Busch began working on Max und Maurice in November 1863. On December 12, he had completed about a hundred drawings, at that time still without verses, which he always wrote after the drawings.

When the Bilderpossen turned out to be a failure, he offered Heinrich Richter the manuscript of Max und Maurice for publication in October 1864, probably as compensation for the financial loss Richter had suffered, waiving any claim to a fee.

Heinrich Richter, however, rejected the manuscript after his father Ludwig Richter had also come to the conclusion that people who took pleasure in such things would not buy books.

So on February 5, 1865, William Busch turned again to his old publisher Kaspar Braun:

»Mein lieber Herr Braun! ... Ich schicke Ihnen nun hier die Geschichte von Max und Moritz, die ich zu Nutz und eigenem Plaisir auch gar schön in Farbe gesetzt habe, mit der Bitte, das Ding recht freundlich in die Hand zu nehmen und hin und wieder ein wenig zu lächeln. Ich habe mir gedacht, es ließe sich als eine Art kleine Kinder-Epopöe vielleicht für einige Nummern der fliegenden Blätter ... verwenden.«

»My dear Mr. Braun! ... I am sending you the story of Max and Maurice, which I have beautifully colored for your own pleasure, with the request that you take the book in your hand and smile a little now and then.

I thought it could be used as a kind of small children's epic perhaps for some numbers of the flying leaves, the Fliegende Blätter ...«.

Kaspar Braun sagte noch im Februar 1865 die Veröffentlichung zu und bat Wilhelm Busch lediglich, Texte und Bilder noch einmal zu überarbeiten. Er wollte die Geschichte nicht in den Fliegenden Blättern veröffentlichen, sondern damit das Kinderbuchprogramm des Verlags Braun und Schneider erweitern.Für die Rechte zahlte er Wilhelm Busch einmalig 1000 Gulden. Dies entsprach etwa zwei Jahreslöhnen eines Handwerkers und war für Wilhelm Busch eine stolze Summe.

Im August 1865 zeichnete Wilhelm Busch in München die Geschichte auf Holzdruckstöcke für den Druck mittels Holzstich. Die Vorzeichnung wurde von ihm mit Bleistift auf die grundierten Platten von Hirn- oder Kernholz von Harthölzern übertragen. Jeder Szene der Bildergeschichte entsprach ein bezeichneter Buchsbaumstock.

Der Holzstich ist ein Hochdruckverfahren, das gegen Ende des 18. Jahrhunderts entwickelt und zur meistverwendeten Reproduktionstechnik für Illustrationen wurde. Im Gegensatz zum gröberen Holzschnitt wurde der Druckstock nicht auf weiches Langholz, sondern auf hartes Kernholz übertragen und erlaubte dadurch ähnliche Feinheiten wie der aufwendige und kostenintensive Kupferstich. Kaspar Braun hatte in jungen Jahren die erste Werkstatt in Deutschland gegründet, die mit Holzstich arbeitete.

Zwischen dem Brief von Wilhelm Busch an Kaspar Braun im Februar 1865 und der Veröffentlichung von Max und Moritz vergingen sechs Monate. Die von Wilhelm Busch mit Bleistift auf Buchsbaumholz übertragenen Zeichnungen wurden im Atelier des Verlegers weiterverarbeitet. Was auf dem Druck weiß bleiben sollte, wurde von Facharbeitern mit Sticheln aus der Platte gestochen.

The answer came in the same month. Kaspar Braun agreed to publish the story and merely asked William Busch to revise the texts and pictures. He did not want to publish the story in the Fliegende Blätter, but rather to expand the children's book program of the Braun und Schneider publishing house.

For the rights, he paid William Busch a one-time fee of 1000 guilders. This was equivalent to about two years' wages for a craftsman and was a proud sum for William Busch.

In August 1865, William Busch drew the story in Munich on wooden printing blocks for printing by wood engraving. He transferred the preliminary drawing in pencil onto the primed plates of end-grain of hardwoods. Each scene of the picture story corresponded to a designated boxwood block.

Wood engraving is a letterpress process that was developed towards the end of the 18th century and became the most widely used reproduction technique for illustrations.

Unlike the coarser woodcut, the printing block was transferred to hard heartwood rather than soft longwood, allowing for similar intricacies as the more elaborate and costly copperplate engraving. Kaspar Braun had founded the first workshop in Germany to work with wood engraving at a young age.

Six months passed between William Busch's letter to Kaspar Braun in February 1865 and the publication of Max und Maurice.

The drawings transferred by William Busch in pencil onto boxwood were further processed in the publisher's studio. What was to remain white on the print was engraved from the plate by skilled workers using burins.

Nicht immer entsprach die Arbeit des Holzstechers der Vorzeichnung. Wilhelm Busch ließ einzelne Platten nacharbeiten oder neu anfertigen. Der Holzstich wurde gewöhnlich nur für Schwarz-Weiß-Druck verwendet. Busch hatte aber in seinem Manuskript die meisten Szenen mit zarten Aquarelltönen koloriert. Farbige Ausgaben wurden daher in sogenannten Kolorieranstalten mit Schablonen von Hand ausgemalt, wobei man sich stark an Buschs Manuskriptvorlagen orientierte. Erst ab 1918 kam der Farbendruck zur Anwendung, sodass spätere Auflagen zunehmend bunter wurden und teils sehr lebhaft koloriert sind.

Die Erstausgabe erschien im Oktober 1865 in einer Auflage von 4000 Exemplaren, die sich zunächst nur schleppend verkaufen ließen. Erst ab der zweiten Auflage 1868 verbesserten sich die Verkaufszahlen, und in Buschs Todesjahr 1908 zählte man bereits 56 Auflagen und mehr als 430.000 verkaufte Exemplare.

Für Kaspar Braun und seinen Verlag waren »Max und Moritz« eine wahre Goldgrube. Zum 70. Geburtstag von Wilhelm Busch im April 1902 überwies ihm der Verlag daher ein Geschenk von 20.000 Reichsmark, nach heutiger Kaufkraft etwa 200.000 Euro, die Wilhelm Busch an zwei Krankenhäuser in Hannover spendete.

Max und Moritz gehört heute noch vor dem Struwwelpeter zu den bekanntesten Werken der deutschen Kinderliteratur. Bereits zu Wilhelm Buschs Lebzeiten wurde das Werk in zehn Sprachen übersetzt. 1997 gab es mindestens 281 Übersetzungen in Dialekte und Sprachen.

Außerdem gibt es Parodien, Nachahmungen, Vertonungen, Dramatisierungen und Max-und-Moritz-Plastiken. Seit 1984 wird im Comic-Salon Erlangen der Max-und-Moritz-Preis verliehen.

The wood engraver's work did not always correspond to the preliminary drawing. William Busch had individual plates reworked or newly made.

The wood engraving was usually only used for black and white printing. However, Busch had colored most of the scenes in his manuscript with delicate watercolor tones. Colored editions were therefore hand-painted with stencils in so-called coloring houses, strongly oriented on Busch's manuscript templates.

It was not until 1918 that color printing came into use, so that later editions became increasingly colorful and are sometimes very vividly colored.

The first edition of 4000 copies was published in October 1865 and initially sold only sluggishly. It was not until the second edition in 1868 that sales figures improved, and in 1908, the year of Busch's death, there were already 56 editions and more than 430,000 copies sold.

For Kaspar Braun and his publishing house, »Max und Maurice« was a veritable gold mine. For William Busch's 70th birthday in April 1902, the publisher therefore sent him a gift of 20,000 Reichsmarks, or about 200,000 Euros in today's purchasing power, which William Busch donated to two hospitals in Hanover.

Max und Maurice is still one of the best-known works of German children's literature, ahead of Struwwelpeter. Even during William Busch's lifetime, the work was translated into ten languages. In 1997, there were at least 281 translations into dialects and languages.

There are also parodies, imitations, settings, dramatizations and Max and Maurice sculptures. Since 1984, the Max and Maurice Prize has been awarded at the Comic Salon Erlangen.

Die Deutsche Bundespost brachte 1958 zum 50. Todestag von Wilhelm Busch eine Sondermarke mit Max und Moritz heraus.

Wilhelm Busch hat stets betont, dass er die Bildergeschichte »zu Nutz und eignem Plaisir« verfasst habe. Die saarländische Autorin Edith Braun vertritt jedoch die Auffassung, er habe in »Max und Moritz« einige Ereignisse aus der Zeit der Frankfurter Nationalversammlung 1848/49 verschlüsselt dargestellt. Sein Manuskript, das unter Buschs Münchner Malerfreunden kursierte, enthalte doppeldeutige Botschaften wie doppelte Großbuchstaben, gleiche Buchstaben in unterschiedlicher Form, zwischen die Zeilen geschriebene Wörter und unterschiedliche Formen von Doppelstrichen.

Die Hühner deutet sie als Anspielung auf Heinrich von Gagern, den Präsidenten der Frankfurter Nationalversammlung. Das Rawau! Rawau! des Spitzes im zweiten Streich spiele auf Franz Raveaux an, der Abgeordneter der Frankfurter Nationalversammlung war, wobei sie betont, dass die Spitzel jener Zeit als Spitz bezeichnet wurden. Die Maikäfer seien ein Hinweis auf Philipp Jakob Siebenpfeiffer, der gelegentlich als Großer Kaiser der Mai-Freiheit und Großer Maikäfer des Einen und Ungeteilten Deutschlands verspottet worden sei, usw.

The German Federal Post Office issued a special stamp featuring Max and Maurice in 1958 to mark the 50th anniversary of William Busch's death.

William Busch always emphasized that he had written the picture story »for his own use and plaisir«. The Saarland author Edith Braun, however, holds that in »Max and Maurice« he depicted some events from the time of the Frankfurt National Assembly in 1848/49 in a coded way.

His manuscript, which circulated among Busch's Munich painter friends, contains ambiguous messages such as double capital letters, the same letters in different shapes, words written between the lines, and different forms of double dashes.

She interprets the chickens as an allusion to Heinrich von Gagern, the president of the Frankfurt National Assembly. The Rawau! Rawau! of Spitz in trick second , she says, alludes to Franz Raveaux, who was a member of the Frankfurt National Assembly, emphasizing that the spies of that time were called spitz.

The May bugs, she says, are a reference to Philipp Jakob Siebenpfeiffer, who was occasionally mocked as the Great Emperor of May Liberty and the Great May Bug of the One and Undivided Germany, etc.

Wilhelm Busch war ein ernster und verschlossener Mensch, der viele Jahre seines Lebens zurückgezogen in der Provinz lebte und seinen Bildergeschichten, die ihn berühmt machten, nur wenig Wert beimaß. Er betrachtete sie zu Beginn nur als Broterwerb, mit dem er nach einem abgebrochenen Kunststudium und jahrelanger finanzieller Abhängigkeit von den Eltern seine drückende wirtschaftliche Situation aufbessern konnte. Er suchte zeitlebens nach einer tieferen künstlerischen Erfüllung, als sie ihm seine humoristischen Werke bieten konnten.

Als erster Vorläufer des heute allgegenwärtigen Comics genießt er bleibenden Ruhm, doch sein Traum, ein großer Maler zu werden, erfüllte sich bis zu seinem Tod am 9. Januar 1908 nicht.

Aber kehren wir noch einmal zur Mühle in Ebergötzen zurück, wo sich die beiden Jugendfreunde bis an ihr Lebensende immer wieder trafen. Was geschah dort eigentlich genau mit Max und Moritz? Manche Kritiker glauben, dass die bösen Buben dort ihre verdiente Todesstrafe erhielten. Aber passt das wirklich zu einem Ort, der für Wilhelm Busch mit den schönsten Kindheitserinnerungen verbunden war? Was geschah wirklich im rumpelnden Trichter dieser Mühle?

William Busch was a serious and secretive man who lived many years of his life in seclusion in the provinces and attached little value to his picture stories that made him famous. At the beginning, he regarded them only as a means of earning a living, with which he could improve his oppressive economic situation after years of financial dependence on his parents and abandoning his art studies.

Throughout his life, he searched for a deeper artistic fulfillment than his humorous works could offer him.

He enjoys lasting fame as the first forerunner of the now ubiquitous comic strip, but his dream of becoming a great painter was not fulfilled until his death on January 9, 1908.

But let's return to the mill in Ebergötzen, where the two childhood friends met again and again until the end of their lives. What exactly happened there with Max and Maurice? Some critics believe that the bad boys received their deserved death sentence there. But does that really fit with a place that was associated with the most beautiful childhood memories for William Busch? What really happened in the rumbling hopper of this mill?

Mit der Übeltäterei
War es also nun vorbei,
Doch die Bengel lebten weiter
Wie die Engel hehr und heiter.
Denn in diesem Zaubertrichter
Wurden unsre Bösewichter
Im Getriebe dieser Mühle,
Im Gewalke und Gewühle,
Zwar zerknirscht, zerknackt, zerkleinert,
Blankpoliert, versohlt, verfeinert,
Aber keineswegs zu Mehl! –
Darin geht ihr völlig fehl! –
Schaut doch nur genauer hin!
Der Beschauer schaut den Sinn:

Yes, from great rascality
Now, indeed, the town was free,
But the rascals were not gone,
Both bad boys live on and on.

For inside the mill's great hopper,
In the gears each single flopper,
Grinding body, soul and mind,
Has been polished, crushed, refined,
But this great refining power
Did not grind them into flour!

Just inquire and you see,
What is obvious to me:

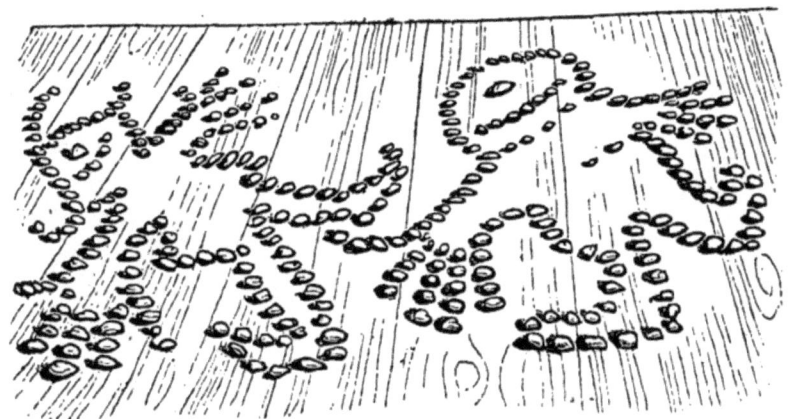

Durch die Eulenspiegelstreiche
Ward aus ihnen eine reiche
Schokoladentalerspeise,
Die wir kurioserweise
Schlucken wie das Huhn den Köder ...
Ach, verflixte Schwerenöter!

Through their Ulenspiegel pranks
They were harvesting big thanks
Fate formed from them chocolate dollars
Which go sweet behind our collars
As into the poultry's throat!
What a dinner! What a load!

Und für Wilhelm Busch, den Maler,
Wurden daraus tausend Taler,
Dem Verleger gar noch mehr.
Solche Speise mundet sehr,
Macht die Leser kerngesund
Und die Schlucker reich und rund!

Oebisfelde, 1. Februar 2022, Jan Müller

And for William Busch, the author
Real gold dollars and further
Even publishers earn money,
And the readers get their honey.
Heavens! Readers heigh and healthy,
And the author fairly wealthy,
By these rascals' form and sound
All are growing rich and round.

Benutzte und zitierte Quellen:
https://de.wikipedia.org/wiki/Max_und_Moritz
https://de.wikipedia.org/wiki/Wilhelm_Busch
https://www.wilhelm-busch-muehle.de

Ein kurzweilig Lesen von

Till Eulenspiegel

aus dem Lande zu Braunschweig

Wie er sein Leben vollbracht hat

Alfa-Veda

Wundersame Reisen und Abenteuer
des Freiherrn von

Münchhausen

Wie er sie bei der Flasche im Kreise
seiner Freunde zu erzählen pflegte

Alfa-Veda

Johann Wolfgang von Goethe

Märchen

Illustriert von
Hermann Hendrich
und Hermann Linde

Alfa-Veda
Bilingual

The Fairy Tale of the Green Snake and the Beautiful Lily

Translated by Thomas Carlyle

Slovenly Peter

German First Print of 1845 by
Heinrich Hoffmann

English Translation by
Mark Twain

Alfa-Veda

Leseproben und Bestellung auf www.alfa-veda.com

Leseproben und Bestellung auf www.alfa-veda.com